A COLLECTION OF SHORT STORIES

RAINBOW

DHARA PARMAR DESAI

First Published in December 2021

ISBN: 978-93-5472-483-1

BLUEROSE PUBLISHERS
www.bluerosepublishers.com
info@bluerosepublishers.com
+91 8882 898 898

Cover Design:
Geetika

Typographic Design:
Jyoti

Distributed by: BlueRose, Amazon, Flipkart

PRELUDE

The intention behind writing this book is to give the readers an experience of fictional short stories comprising of varied ideas of my imagination that would make them undergo several emotions and be a part of each made up fancy. The attempt is to bring together the different forms of lives that probably exist in a slighter or major form around us. To propagate the strength people, gather after the ups and downs in their lives and yet yearn to live happily or find delight in their existing lives. Hope my work makes you smile after each tale and leaves you at ease.

Regards,

Dhara Parmar Desai.

ACKNOWLEDGEMENT

To the most valuable treasure I possess, now and after life.

Mom and Dad

****

To my constant supporter

My Significant Other
Kiral Desai

****

To the creator of beautiful and profound illustrations

Rutika Deshpande

****

Contents

AAJIMA

AAJIMA

Aajima - The most known, matured and experienced woman in the Ghosh Family. Beginning with the designing of the house and the menu of the food, it all needed aver of her word. Seemed the family was so dependent on her actions and decisions, a day without Aajima would toss it all to a messy scene.

The Ghosh's – comprised of two sons from Aajima and Naren Ghosh named Satish the first one and Subrato as the second. Both married, settled and lined their family with two kids each. The elder wife (Shona) passed her days in an utter discontentment of not being able to have a nuclear family. With her kids Roshni and Koyal she tried to form her own separate castle of unfulfilled desires hoping to fulfill them some day. The younger one (Haldi) always seemed to be in her own creation of imaging herself as an actress. Nurturing the two twin toddlers seemed a burden to her. Above all this, a silent, always helping and submissive voice just sought peace in the residence and that was Mr. Ghosh.

Aajima with her royalty and tact had the family well knit. As the family like any other had been building stability in expected areas due to Aajima's and Narenji's efforts, a shock withheld it all back.

Narenji, the patriarchal support and the eldest member of the family succumbed to a severe heart attack. More than the sons and the daughters-in-law, Aajima felt the excruciating pain of his loss. Now, being ` the head of the family, she took the total charge of all that needed attention. She yet had that powerful and esteemed legacy in her tone and thoughts.

As a few months passed Shona created a typical family drama seeking a private life with her family. "I want to live my life now on my own terms and conditions. I want to move out of this scheduled life and have a nuclear family", said Shona to Satish and other members noticing her tantrums. Looking at the unexpected rift, Subrato seized the moment, which meant they wanted to put up a similar idea. Once Shona was done, Aajima just rolled her eyes towards Satish expecting he would at least speak a word of concern in his Maa's favour, but he just looked down adding to his wife's voice.

That night Aajima sat alone in the arm chair lost in her thoughts and remembering Narenji's words, "Our duty as parents is over. We have got the kids settled; they have the best of their lives. Some day they would want to change their lives. Their lives, which might not have us in it". Saying this Narenji held Aajima's hand and smiled. But Aajima never thought her kids could ever be happy without her.

But that night Aajima could see Narenji's words getting valid. Very soon the house was just a place to accommodate, cook, bathe, eat and sleep for the sons. Aajima sensed that Subrato too displayed traits which sought freedom, freedom from Aajima's responsibility. Her identity was getting faded within months of her husband's death.

Finally, a day came when at the Dinner table Satish with a little lower voice says, "Maa we had planned for immigration to the States some time ago and the good news is we have made it and the entire family will be soon migrating to US." Satish couldn't face the eyeballs of his mother awaiting contact. Aajima added, "The entire family? Oh, so I think I can come too right?" She smiled in a pouring sadness because she knew the silence of her son was a NO. Everyone then departed to their rooms when Aajima's room knocked. "Maa, you awake?" It was Subrato. "Oh, yes! Son", come in. Aajima felt loved again. She thought she had some hope on her younger one which she still had. "Maa, actually me and Haldi wanted to tell you something. She got a modeling offer in Mumbai, Maa, so we plan on shifting there in a month's time. I shall too find some good earning there as I'm very fascinated by the city. As soon as Aajima heard this, a stretched smile dragged back to a sunken look. Sons who she thought would never ignore or neglect her are now getting too selfish. They are thinking practically. They are leaving her alone. None of the two had even expressed a slightest gesture of asking or seeking her company.

Aajima rolled the beads of her mala that night and sobbed in loneliness. She longed a hug, a pat, a word of affection that could soothe her ailing soul. With a heavy heart Aajima passed that night. She had a terrible disliking for those who slouched and sulked sitting on their problems and did nothing to breakthrough them. Her children turned out to be henpecked husbands for whom their wedded wives and children were the actual responsibility and the bearer in her womb for nine months was an excess baggage and encumbrance. Aajima had expected at this junction of her life that at least one of the offspring could show a symbol of chivalry or maternal respect. But here she found them proving her wrong.

Satish and Subrato had finally left the Ghosh residence, secluding Aajima to survive her coming years in a way totally opposite of that she had dreamt of. It wasn't going well for her to cope up or rather accept the bitter reality that she's now all by her own till she lived. She had given up all hopes on her sons who she thought would have been beside her when Narenji is not.

A FEW MONTHS LATER...

One fine breezy morning, Aajima made up her mind to get herself out of the stress stricken life that ruled her. She had great interest in ancient languages and its profound studies. A Language Club had begun in a hyper local premise near her domicile. Through a dear friend she enrolled herself and began to visit the club regularly. The first few sessions helped her make a rapport with other people who took part in the club. Eventually, Aajima realized that the Club premises became her morale booster classes. She would write poetries in Sanskrit, read other books and she became so busy and occupied she never had time for her woes. Meanwhile, when Aajima would be sitting and chatting with her club friends, the sons wouldn't get lucky to have their calls answered. She had accepted that her life was much more above children who have now turned to be selfish humans against her selfless love.

One Sunday afternoon the Language Club had chosen the Ghosh's mansion to gather for a Tea party where all the students, young, mediocre, old had summed to make it a memorable one. Rekha, one of Aajima's close companion calls her out loudly, "Aaji, Aaji, look here" Dragging Aajima from an ongoing conversation, Rekha introduces her to a tall, well built, handsome, gentleman with pepper salt hair pairing the same age as Aajima's. "She is Aaji my friend I keep telling you about and how well-versed and known she is about her language". And Aaji this is Mr. Shekhar who has come down from US to, I'm sorry but he lost his wife a month ago so he has been here to fulfill the rituals but now he is fine and knows he needs to move on for his own self. His wife was from here (Kolkata)", said Rekha. Aajima interrupted the talk and expressed sorrow to Mr. Shekhar on his deep loss. "It's been a month now that Mona is no more, I'm trying to gain my peace and stability by joining this Club as I find it has a therapeutic value, what do you feel?" asked Shekhar to Aajima. But Aaji had already woven her thoughts to the past memories with Narenji on the mention of Mona. A sudden shake from Rekha got her back with a jerk. "I'm sorry, I was just in thoughts." said Aajima. "I understand and empathize to your state. I know it all about you and your life in present and past, through Rekha. I appreciate your vitality and derring-do way to welcome life. I'm not flattering you here nor being caustic. It's just pure pride I gift you to wear it as a crown." saying this Mr. Shekhar looked at Aajima with an innocent look awaiting an assertion from her. Taking a few more seconds Aajima quickly glanced at Mr. Shekhar who still watched her Beauty and her lean face, her Big round Bindi and a fringe resting down her cheek which she kept settling behind her ears again and again. She then looked at Rekha, smiled and hugged her. With this Rekha proposed that she actually forgot to tell her there is a supper party at Narenji's house that day itself.

"Yes, I should personally give you a warm word of invitation to make your presence possible. It will be my pleasure", said Mr. Shekhar. Aajima a little apprehensively said, "Thanks but..." Rekha interrupted her and said, "Shekharji, she has endless alibis to make, I promise she will tag with me." Aajima helplessly looked at Rekha and thanked Mr. Shekhar for such a homely response.

It was almost evening and Aajima had spread all her best saris and jewellery on the bed unable to decide and choose on the Best. With the rush she again droops into her thoughts, "This Emerald necklace is adding beauty to itself as its set around your neck Aaji. You look so beautiful", saying this Narenji sticks a big bindi on Aajima's forehead symbolizing that she is ready. A sudden cacophonous ringtone drags her back and its Rekha seeking her to be ready. She breathes in sigh and wears a Black crushed cotton silk sari with a high neck blouse and a loose bun, a diamond necklace and bangles accompanied with a matched brocade clutch. The horn honked and Rekha was right there to pick her up.

In a while they reached Mr. Shekhar's, an equally posh Bungalow or should be called a castle, a humungous space ahead as a drive through and a special chauffeur who took the courtesy to park the cars. As we climbed the stairs that led to a vintage door with sag wood, perfectly uniformed men who came forth to welcome the guests and showed them way to the party hall. As we entered we saw Mr. Shekhar holding a glass of champagne with delicacy and enjoying it in little sips and exchanged smiles with his guests. He had immense chivalrous approach for the females too. He softly shook hand with them and treated them with so much respect. It felt a man like this would never be a victim of male chauvinism.

"Aaji, come let's go meet him", forced Rekha.

"Rekha you begin. I shall join; I have a few known ladies to see since long."

Aajima spoke hesitantly. But Rekha took her to Mr. Shekhar. "Shekharji, Namaste, see I told you, I'll fetch her along. Here she is", said Rekha.

Aajima, shy and sheepish smiled with courtesy and all her goodness but couldn't hide her discomfort. She never felt this for a very long time. Her throat was thickening and her heart was pounding. She could feel moisture in her hands and with all this physical turbulence she rebelled it and grew her face to Mr. Shekhar who waited in anticipation to have a sight of

Aajima's face and her Beauty. His looks gave Aaji a sudden goose pimpled feeling and collywobbles in her stomach. She exchanged a look with a smile and shook hand with him. As the action was ongoing Mr. Shekhar uttered, "I should indeed confess with not word to lie, Aaji you look very beautiful tonight. I couldn't resist myself from saying this." Aajima expressed gratitude and dispatched her hand from his. By then Rekha had been busy with her other folks. The duo now had some solace to talk more and share.

The day since they met it seemed they shared a deep liking for each other which Mr. Shekhar didn't hesitate to exhibit but Aajima prevented those feelings and suppressed their expression. Deep inside she had started finding peace and joy in his company. She liked when he praised her. She wanted to look good again make herself up, dress up, smile, go out. It was all him. She knew she wanted to go ahead with him but she was scared of becoming a maudlin, as she was in case of her children. She did not have any allowance of an obnoxious incident that could shatter her life completely. While she was battling with her thoughts suddenly Mr. Shekhar holds her hand and takes her to a huge open balcony which had a graceful view of the night and the city.

"I'm scared of the dark Aaji, I'm a man yet I'm scared. I can see that fear in your eyes too. Fear of losing your loved ones again, fear that you might fall in love again, what if it doesn't work. What if I'm hurt again? There is no answer to all this Aaji. I kept on pondering all this through my life but I lost many people, things, money, and my wife. But I stood up, lived again; smiled and learnt what is gone shall never come back until it's destined to be. Be happy with what you possess, who you have and not be a sullen by brooding over what is gone and when will it return. Nothing is certain and permanently ongoing, not even we as humans. Hold on to what and who are yours and the rest shall fall in place. With this consoling speech a heart pouring realization along with affection was seen in Aajima and she fell into Mr. Shekhar's arms and cried to the depth of her sorrows, loneliness, loss of her children's love and Narenji. In this course her phone was ringing for quite some time and when she saw Satish calling she didn't care enough to attend it.

Now, there was a silence between the two and each waited for the other to utter a word and then Aajima finally looks at Mr. Shekhar wipes her eyes and says, "Thanks." Mr. Shekhar pats her back and with a soothing gesture proposes saying, "Come with me to US, I shall be beside you when you look next, I promise to return the joys you felt had lost forever. Have faith in me.

Aajima then calls Satish and he had an array of complaints for his mother since she never answered their calls or cared enough to know how they had been.

"Satish hold on for a minute, I have to inform you something really essential." said Aajima.

"What is it Maa? Have we to suffer any more then please keep us uninformed." Satish added. "Don't worry, Son. It's just about me. I'm coming to States very soon." informed Aajima." What? States? When this happened Maa? Maa we are already struggling since we have had Subrato's family here for vacations, an addition will split our finances and we might not be able to take care of you properly. And..." Aajima interrupted him and said, "Satish, Relax, You needn't worry about taking care of me", Now Aajima had her call audible to Mr. Shekhar too. "I will be all by myself. I have found my way of life and happiness. I wish you and Subrato a happy life ahead too. I will talk later." Desperate enough to know how is Aajima going to make such a big leap in her life, Satish hastily frames, "Maa, but at least tell us who are you going to be with. What are you going to do? Maa are you there? Aajima glanced at Mr. Shekhar and they exchanged a true smile displaying how content they were in each other's company and she hung up the call.

Satish and Subrato kept calling but never got an answer.

Mr. Shekhar and Aajima stood under the twilight and took a deep breath and just kept silent and enjoyed the peace of one another's presence.

****

BIJLI AKA POOJA

BIJLI AKA POOJA

Chameli enters the room. "Bijli your client should be here in next ten minutes time so be ready and just set up the place and yes put a Gajra and a Maroon lipstick, add some tinge of a few sprays of that strong premium mogra freshener. He needs too much of mogra seems." Chameli laughs out, winks at Bijli and leaves. Bijli while removing her earrings and undoing her hair keeps that fake smile on her face and gazes at her make-up so jazzy and gaudy, so much like to suit her profession, an escort, a high end prostitute.

Bijli had never thought she would be dressing up so pompous until she was in her wedding sari after all she belonged to Delhi where marriages were a dream come true and a historical event.

"I won't marry a guy out of Delhi. Seriously, it's very important to have the right kind of chemistry and tuning you know and more than that it becomes so easy if the two belong to the same culture and place.

What do you say, Natasha?" "Well, I agree to your ways to an extent but I have a fascination to marry a big man, a man with a big bungalow, cars, servants, maids and all that any celebrity would live with", exclaimed Natasha in excitement. Giggling and expressing Pooja said, "Firstly, make a proper face to suit a guy like one else you will get all that you said but there could be a little compromise you'll have to make, the man would be a little squint". Natasha starts beating her and they have a fun side to the talk.

Bijli was still in front of the mirror and remembering those days with Natasha and feeling immense nostalgia and knowing the fact that it's too late to do anything about her existence after all that she had been through. Bijli was now set for her next client. Her chastity was no more an example people would give to others to get inspired from. She had given away all her shyness, modesty, sensitivity to a form which demanded just the opposite.

The Door knocks, "Bijli?"

"Yes, I am here. Please come in." The door opened and she was a taken a little aback to see her client. He seemed to be hardly in his youth or may be just inaugurated it.

"Hi, my name is Purab. I paid to be with you and..."

Bijli laughs out and interrupts his introduction, "How did you manage to make the amount I charge is what makes me wonder and you look like you have just grown a few hair sprouts on your chin and upper lip. Are you sure you are at the right place? I guess you are not. Go back kid."

Bijli turns and as she advances to walk further. Purab says, "No. I haven't come to return back this early."

Bijli walks towards him and holds his arm. "Sit and tell me what made you come here?"

"I have had a break up and I'm not able to come out of the thoughts that it's all over now. I know all of it yet it's difficult for me to move on. My friends said I should try another relationship but it's surely too early so they thought I should go for a change and they forced me to come here and I know I am not a kind of boy but I couldn't refuse them no matter how awkward their scheme is and money I have enough as I belong to a rich family. I'm not ready for this and I know my friends want me to be fine but this is not my way."

Bijli calmly looks at Purab and says," You are right Purab. You shouldn't do anything that's not your way. This life wasn't my way too dear, I didn't wish to be what I am but I had to choose this way that was not my way. Don't worry you could stay, talk to me and take the money back. You will need it to treat your friends." "You mean you understand what I'm going through? I'm thankful to you Bijli. I'm so thankful. But can I ask you something? Why did you choose to be here? You seem very different." Bijli smiles and says, "It's a long story Purab, I just want you to grab a lesson from me and leave and that is, live with who makes you happy and do what makes you happy. Rest the world anyway goes on, with or without us." Saying this Bijli pats his cheeks and gives him a tight hug.

"Bijli, I'm so glad I made this decision to come and see you. I'm feeling better and light and I now carry a totally different image about you. Trust me; I feel I found a friend in you. Thanks, Bijli stops him from speaking by placing her hand on his lips. "That's enough! Just smile and be happy. Bye Purab."

Purab left with a light heart but he triggered all that happened in her past that she tried running away from, each and every day. Bijli lied on her bed like a lifeless body recollecting how she became Bijli from Pooja.

"Pooja, did you fetch your Tiffin for college? And you are already late. Natasha is here since half an hour now." shouted Pooja's mother Sushiladevi.

Sushiladevi was a perfect housewife, a loving mother of an only daughter from Vishwanath Sukanya. The family had been living in greater Noida, Delhi, since a decade now. They were Simple, Happy and prosperous Sukanyas. They had all that took to have a peaceful life.

Pooja was growing up too. She had just begun her graduation period and she was very smart, intelligent but above all these qualities nobody could overlook the charm and good looks she possessed. She was blessed with a flawless skin, an even tone, dark black silky hair, eyes quite spherical and so expressive, and cheek bones protruding when she smiled, a body that can be termed as perfect and physically endowed one. She was a god's creation in Leisure.

"Pooja, how long do you take, we missed the first lecture, girl." sighed Natasha.

"Oh, I'm sorry let's rush before we miss the other. Bye Amma, Bye Daddy."

"Bye Beta", yelled the parents.

As soon as the two enter the college, arguing with each other, a boy approaches Pooja abruptly and introduces himself, "Hi, my name is Raghuveer. We are batch mates. You might not know me but I do." Saying this he proposes on a handshake with Pooja. "We are the biggest gang here, not everyone is around but I can introduce you to my dear buddy Dhruv."

" Hey Dhruv, come here. We have a new friend." Dhruv comes close to see Pooja a little submissive and not willing to go ahead with the entire friend thing that was going on. But Dhruv assures a sober approach by mildly shaking hand with her.

"Hi, I'm Dhruv", "I'm Pooja and she is Natasha. It was nice to meet you both; we are already running late for our lectures. Thanks, Bye. Let's go Natasha."

It was obvious that Pooja had seen no male company around for a long time in her life except her father and a few maternal and paternal cousins with whom she wasn't too close or attached. Her life and world revolved only around her parents and Natasha.

The next day Pooja accidentally gets Dhruv as a next bencher and to her surprise, Dhruv was not at all a punk, mischievous or to have an aversion for. He treated her really well, made her comfortable, solved her doubts and gave her a constant assurance that Raghuveer was a nice guy.

"Raghuveer belongs to a very High class family, Pooja. He is very possessive about his things, people and friends. He has had everything before he could dream of it. He is the only son to his parents and he is a very close friend. I control him you could say" smiles Dhruv.

"That's nice but the way he approached me was a little scary. I haven't faced a guy like this ever so I was nearly shivering but now I'm fine and at ease after you came forth and I appreciate you.", saying this Pooja gives a long stare at Dhruv but Dhruv afraid of his emotional quotient avoids it and adds in between, "Uhh... Pooja, let's go to the rock steps behind the college. I have to tell you something." "Natasha, I'll see you after the break" and departs with a smile at her.

It was becoming evident that Pooja was building the first step of liking towards Dhruv. She was feeling a haven with him and she was confident of her safety. She began to trust him.

"So tell me what is it that you wanted to tell me Dhruv", with a smile Pooja looked at him. "I don't know if it's the right time, I know according to me it's too early to have said this but Pooja, Raghuveer has passed his deep liking for you. He wants to have you as his girl. I know he is a little different but he likes you a lot and so I have brought you here." Saying this Dhruv turns to the wall and asks Raghuveer to join.

It wasn't that Raghuveer was shy but he had been engaged in other stuff so saving on his energy and expression he made Dhruv the intermediary.

Now, the trio was face to face. As Pooja looks at Raghuveer she starts hyperventilating and sensed that she is trapped. She hastily began walking through the rocks where Raghuveer stops her and asks what her answer was for his proposal and that she understood how much he liked her beauty. Pooja tries to free her thin and fragile wrist off his heavy, macho fist and with tears in her eyes she looks with scorn at Dhruv and then looks back to Raghuveer. With all her might she frees herself and pounces over Raghuveer with a tight slap and worst of her anger and denies his proposal. By the end of this the entire gang had gathered there inclusive of Natasha. The girls then ran way home as quickly as they could before Raghuveer did anything to make up for his humiliation in front of others.

With deep sobs Pooja confessed to Natasha that night when she stayed with Pooja, "I never expected this from Dhruv, I thought he was going to express his emotions and not in turn be a mediator for his sick friend. I just hate both of them Natasha and she put her head in Natasha's lap and mourned.

The next morning while Pooja and Natasha were about to get ready for their start for the day, they happen to find something really shocking. Their mobile phones were loaded with images from different numbers which had Pooja in her most natural form. It was tact of technology where the body of someone's is merged with someone else's face. Just then Pooja gets a phone call and as she answers it with a Hello she gets the most shocking revert. "Hi, how much do you charge per night? Are you available during the day too? If yes, please book my appointment. I'm interested in you." This was some random man who thought like all those men who called Pooja and wanted the same thing.

Pooja pressed her mouth with her hands unaware of what was going on. Tears never stopped and just then Natasha calls Dhruv and starts yelling, "What do you think you are doing with Pooja, Dhruv? You and your friend have ruined her life. We never expected you people will go this extent following her rejection. She is getting calls from men who want to sleep with her. She is being portrayed as a prostitute, Dhruv.

Dhruv completely out of this, expressed a great shock," WHAT? Natasha? Have you lost your mind? Why would we do that and where is Pooja please let me talk to her." "NO," exclaims Natasha. "Your friend Raghuveer along with his other pervert friends has made obscene images of Pooja and now it's circulating everywhere. Pooja just got a message from him saying, now you shall know, Raghuveer never accepts refusal." and she sobs.

"Natasha, I care for Pooja, I really don't know anything of it. Please let me once talk to Pooja."

As Natasha hands over the phone to Pooja, before Dhruv would speak anything, Pooja said, "Dhruv, I loved you and I know you feel for me as well. But now my career, family, life is shattered to pieces. I thank you for it equally. Now that I'm dragged into this filthy business of perversion about me and my image; I would choose this profession that Raghuveer created for me and I thank you for it equally. Do visit me someday. I won't refuse you, Goodbye, Dhruv."

"Pooja, Relax, please don't do anything of a sort, Pooja listen to me, are you hearing me." But the phone was now turned off.

Within a few days of this disaster, Pooja started facing humiliation from her parents, other family members intervened the happening and taunted and mocked at her parents asking them to re check their upbringing. Everything was messed up. Natasha no more visited her except once when she decided to shift to Mumbai. She shared with Natasha that was the best thing to do for herself and her family. She has no career now, no family, and no friends. She tried ways to get a job from her place itself but it didn't work out and so finally after many attempts she decided to give up on the so called longing for a respectful job and makes up her mind to be a High-end call girl in Mumbai and when she confesses this in front of Natasha, she cried loudly and Pooja just hugged her with dry eyes.

It was then before a year that Pooja entered this profession and used Bijli to hide her real self and name.

"Bijli, Bijli?" Chameli not getting a revert barges in the room and shakes Bijli off her nightmare, the real nightmare she faced while she was in all her senses.

"I'm sorry, I went off to sleep. I was a little unwell." said Bijli.

"That's fine. Now, that you are awake and fresh should I send the other client? He seems too desperate to meet you. He had an appointment in the evening but he is here in the waiting lounge since hours now. You are becoming quite wanted girl. He is all the way from Delhi you know?" said Chameli.

"Delhi? What is his name you said?" "He didn't want to disclose the name to you, it's just a few more minutes. Why don't you wait a little and know for yourself?" "OK. Send him in." said Bijli.

The door then remained opened and not known of someone's footsteps entering the room, Bijli just stands up, turns and rushes into a male figure, broad, tall, her eyes stuck on the chest and when she raises her head up she had a collision with her thoughts and eye sight to see that the man was no one else but Dhruv. He was still the same. Angelic, clear eyed, innocent and benevolent. They could keep sinking into each other's beam forever.

"Pooja, Pooja?" called Dhruv.

"Huh!" uttered Bijli. "I'm not Pooja, my name is Bijli and I don't know you. Let me do my work and you just leave." Saying this Bijli was constantly hiding her eye contact.

"Pooja, Don't fool yourself. Do you have any clue how long it took for me to look for you these months? I haven't been able to do anything with peace after you left abruptly. Raghuveer is no more in Delhi. The entire family shifted abroad. People got the real clue that you were victimized of a sick scheme. I had cut off all contacts with Raghuveer after what he did to you. Pooja, I came here with a hope to show that you are still loved and needed. Your parents were in touch with me always. They trust me now and want that you should go back to them and they wouldn't mind if you want to change the city. But please come back with Me." requested Dhruv.

Pooja not moved by a word and quite stern in her looks said, "It's too late for all this Dhruv and I'm completely a changed person now. I have money in loads. I'm glad I did not study further; no career would give me this earning. I have everything a person would wish to possess for a lavish life. Emotions no more hold any place in the profession I have chosen. I told you when I left. Do come to meet me someday and I'll not refuse you. Bijli is a woman of words. So go ahead."

As she tries to strip her sari off, Dhruv stops her and with the helplessness in his eyes holds Bijli tightly and hugs her and cries his heart out.

"Pooja please don't do this to me. Irrespective of what happened, what you are now, I just want you to be with me. I have come a long way in this journey to find you. You are still the same, shy, pure, prettiest and truthful Pooja for me. I can ignore, forget and shun all that is your present. Just understand how much I need you and how much more I could love you if I have you around me."

With this tender confession Dhruv views Bijli in constancy with those pitiable moist eyes. After a prolonged gaze, Bijli sheds tears and throws herself on the floor holding Dhruv's legs tightly. Dhruv not interrupting her, lets her have the outburst till emptiness. He then holds her, leads her up and hugs her, consoles her caressing her hair and rubbing her wet eye-balls.

Bijli had now felt she had someone who belonged to her completely. She quits on her profession and the couple finds a new way to life —Chennai.

****

TETE - A -TETE

TETE-A-TETE

"Seasons are so exclusive. They arrive when it's their turn. They need no alarm, no intimation, and no calls. Nature rules them and the pair works greatly, today we have proved to be a great pair too. All of us. We have teamed up and worked for best results and outcomes. So let's be the Seasons and our Nature the Singhania Industries, rule. Ladies and Gentlemen today on this great opening of our new venture, I, Aaditya Singhania want to congratulate all of you for making this happen. For helping us expand in such a quick pace. Thank you all and now I'd like to mention with all my deep gratitude within, the founder of Singhania Industries, My Father Mr. Suraj Singhania to come ahead and share this success with us. With these words the hall was filled with a round of applause appreciating Aaditya and Suraj Singhania, the son and the father. Mr. Singhania climbed the stairs and hugged his son tightly and congratulated his success for expanding the Business. There they stood proud and vain in front of a jam-packed staff accepting their good work with dignity.

But before this who knew what would have led Aaditya Singhania to be one.

He was Aaditya in the past too but from a different family. He belonged to a mediocre family which had a father, mother and he as a son. Aaditya's Father Vinod Bhat and mother Sheena Bhat worked hard and earned money to give their son a decent life. The three of them lived in the city while the rest of them resided in their village homes. Things were fine until Aaditya got the news of his parents' car accident of which they did not survive. Ramcharam the most loyal friend to Vinod brought the news and informed the family lineage as well so that they could move further with the formalities and rituals. By then Aaditya was in his early mid age. As per the tradition the family, folks and relatives visited and fulfilled the kriya karm and stayed with Aaditya for a week or two and handed him to Ramcharan and flee back to their lives. By the time Aaditya could even understand that he had lost his parents and that they were never going to come back and that there was no one he could depend on, he just kept mourning about his great loss. He was too young to educate himself for years ahead. With some money from his parents' accounts, Ramcharan managed to pay his fees and get him his basic needs. But all that was not enough to feed him for a longer time. With the passing days Aaditya in his tender age and mind realized that none of his relatives and other family members would take his responsibility. So he had to be strong and find a way to survive and get through this toughest time of life. He was extremely hurt and had no vision to move further in which direction. But all he could do was show extreme maturity and do something to get back to normality and earn some living. Destiny took him to a level of degradation and loneliness. All he wanted was to survive now and take care of his basic needs. Looking at his grievous state Ramcharam laid a helping hand to him and set him up as a helper at a decent firm for ground level tasks. One day while it was a normal working day for everyone, Aaditya was not oblivious of the drastic change his life was going to be in. Mr. Singhania, the sole owner of a series of chemical machinery industries paid a visit to his current small firm just to check the working pace. While exploring the regular mechanism, he kept on constantly noticing Aaditya's dedication towards his basic and simple job. Mr. Singhania was truly impressed by the boy's passion to do the smallest task with deep sincerity.

Ramcharan detailed Mr. Singhania with the events that transformed Aaditya's life and how to help himself he worked hard and did this job.

Mr. Singhania became the godfather for Aaditya. One fine day, Ramcharan packs all his available baggage and takes him to a huge Bungalow which had all service class people but only one man to be served, Ramcharan had convinced Aaditya to come along with him and on the way he comes to know that he has been adopted as a son by one of the richest man of the city of Dehradun. It took time and patience for him to neutrally treat the drastic makeover of his life. Gradually, the two became best of company for one another and they healed each other's woes. More than a Father-Son bond they had a human bonding and attachment. The past and fresh memories of both of them kept sticking to their hearts like a smallest feather to our finger.

On a Sunday morning the two were sipping their fresh tea and Mr. Singhania couldn't resist his expression and said, "Aaditya, I'm happy that I met you. I feel my burden is totally vanished. I'm fortunate to have you as my partner, my friend, my son. Thanks dear."

"Dad, you need not speak it all, your actions do it. I should be the one saying all that and I want to relieve you of all your responsibilities and retire you to a peaceful life. The Business is under a positive check. Well, that reminds me I have a road journey for a land analysis somewhere in the interior of Bilaspur which could be really profitable purchase for our production process.

"Why do you want to drag yourself so much? I shall send someone to sanction the place and finish further formalities. You could just be here and have some time off for yourself."

Mr. Singhania proposed. "No, Dad. For me every task or business is important. So please allow me to continue. Moreover, I'm going to return by later evening and that still gives me enough time to stretch in peace."

While the discussion came to a mutual conclusion, Aaditya asked his chauffer to get ready for the travel in an hour's time. Once the journey began, Aaditya gets time to see the fields they crossed by. He could see the closer trees moving along with him in speed and those farther in distance moving slowly in an opposite direction. This was awkward as he noticed and found so much of similarity in the relations in his life. The farther things he related to were his past family and the closer ones as his present. Aaditya was very practical now. He had no time or space for anything that motivated helplessness and a longing to answer all unanswered questions. Aaditya was now a man with big dreams, pure heart, philanthropy, humanity and one who lived to make a difference. All that he had borne in the past was where it was supposed to be. The present and new life was something worth a fortune which might not end even after he leaves the world.

Lost in all these thoughts, Aaditya just nods his head to himself and asks the chauffeur, "How long do we still have to travel Shiva? It's almost been a while since we have been travelling now."

Before Shiva could reciprocate to the query, the car made a screeching sound and stopped with a sudden jerk. Trying to figure out what the matter was, Shiva and Aaditya get down and find to their distress that the car was punctured.

"Oh! Gosh. Is this the place it was supposed to happen?" Aaditya looks around turning his head and finding only a few Lorries on the track, trees around and just behind them a

Dhaba named Sita Ram. It was a basic set up like a Big cubical which had woven beds in the open space before one enters the Dhaba. The time was just welcoming sunset and there were few scattered beds which had small tables placed in its front to serve the customers. While Shiva was trying to contact the road assistance to help them get back on road, they declared it was a little difficult for them to come very sooner. Now the two were handicapped. By the time they could decide on anything, Aaditya makes up his mind to leave the next early morning.

Now that the stress of returning back was low, Aaditya takes a chance to relieve him and informs Mr. Singhania about the issue and that he chose to stay there that night and that he shouldn't bother. In the middle of his telephonic conversation a little boy, mostly in his growing age catches his attention. Aaditya found something so familiar and eye catching about him that he took up the most comfortable bed and comforted one leg on the other and just enjoyed the service the boy paid to all the truck drivers. He would run to them with a towel and a pitcher of water and once they are done splashing their face with it, he would offer them a towel to pat dry. Everyone he went to patted his back or offered a small tip as a reward to his quick service. Running back to get the tea kettle with a smile he felt proud for what he earned was much more valuable than money.

Aaditya could sense the relativity of his past with this boy's present. He was constantly curious to know everything about this boy. What made him do this kind of work? Where he belonged to? Is he happy with this life and work? With the collision of so many thoughts in his mind, Aaditya is deeply engrossed in them and he doesn't realize a voice calling out for him.

"Saab, Saab? O Saab!".

"Oh!" said Aaditya with a shock as if someone splashes water on your face while you dreaming and lose track of it. "Yes You? What is your name? He asked the Boy.

The Boy was a little excited to answer back as he knew how to converse in English. But the kind of place he was at, nobody would even use English words in bits. "My name is Bhanu, Saab. This is not my real name but here they call me Bhanu because I work here." Before Aaditya could reply his answer Bhanu got a little stressed and worried with a voice husky and boisterous who demanded him to go back to the kitchen and work. He ran with all his might leaving a little sand dust in the air.

Aaditya realized Bhanu was badly frightened of his master. From that little incident he could also make out of some undiscovered loopholes of his life. He felt that Bhanu was either forced to do this work or else he had no option. Bhanu seemed a handsome boy with a fair skin most of which hid due to the extreme tanning from the heat he worked in. Aaditya couldn't ignore the dark circles underneath his eyes which revealed the boy couldn't enjoy an eight-hour sleep. While he kept brooding about Bhanu, Shiva intervenes and asks Aaditya not to be at this place as it was a normal stand by Dhaba that offers just some snacks, fix thali, packet junk and some beverages which doesn't suit anywhere to his level. But Aaditya asks Shiva not to worry about his comfort and asks him to go ahead and have something to eat and take some rest as they had to return tomorrow.

The Dhaba was now a quiet place as not many lorry drivers occupied it. Glancing the place, Aaditya again notices Bhanu cleaning the floor and setting things to its place. He was placing the beverage bottles so close in perfection as if they were ready to parade. Small packets of cookies so well placed in a row tugged with each other with plastic covers of yellow, orange, green, pink as if forming a free design in a kaleidoscope. As he watched this, Bhanu and Aaditya look at each other and Bhanu places the dry mop on his shoulder and waves to Aaditya. To which he summons Bhanu to him.

"So, you every day work so hard Bhanu?"

"Yes Saab"

"Hold on Bhanu. Don't call me Saab. Instead you can call me Bhaiya. How does it sound to you?".

Bhanu smiles at Aaditya and nods his head and now he was so excited to tell him more about himself as he felt close with him.

"Yes Bhaiya, I work hard as I have no other thing to do. I like playing cricket but it is not possible here so I don't play and working here gets me food and place to sleep so I have to."

Bhaiya what do you do? Tell me about your life too, what work you do? Your clothes and car look very nice so you must be very rich, Right Bhaiya?"

Bhanu kept looking at Aaditya waiting to hear from him about his journey of life and seemed that Aaditya couldn't resist telling Bhanu about his life too but he held back his excitement as he still had a little more span with Bhanu knowing him.

"Forget about it Bhanu, I have to ask a few more questions to you before you totally skip your night's sleep. So you speak such good English, how come, are you trained or you learnt it through practice?" "Bhaiya, I studied till standard 5th in an English medium school and that is how I know English." And how I reached here in life is even more tragic and unreal to believe if told."

"What is it? Would you mind sharing?"

"No I wouldn't mind sharing Bhaiya."

"It just began when we had shifted to this new home in somewhere near Haridwar. I was upset because we left my better home previously and my dear school as well, my friends, my teachers, everything. As we were now close to our other relatives my parents were quite happy thinking their kids could be a better company for me in this new surrounding but how do they know how much I hated them and how much they bullied me when they visited us. It was just after our moving that my cousins and family visited us at our new home. They were annoying and I never liked them. But we used to play with each other as it made the family gatherings less boring. Moreover, they were also too jealous of me and envied my brains and skills. They all pranked me always. So that day, unaware of the fact that they had some knowledge of this place, I agreed on searching a new place to play and began following them not realizing we reached too far from our home inside some aloof barren land. I had a clue I am fine until I was with them since they got me to this place. I still insisted on returning and playing close to the house as it was safe but they took me into trust and we began playing hide and seek and as they planned I was the ill lucked one to count till at least a 100. Once I was done, I found they all had practically left me alone to this deserted and lone place where I was a total alien. Initially knowing it's a game I somehow used my energy searching them everywhere possible but in vain. Of course, since it was a scheme to mislead me. I started panicking now as it was too early for me to remember the lanes, landmarks to return as I wasn't trained to come this far from my family and my home. I was running to get some help from the small road that took my attention and it seemed to be connecting the city. I was running out of Breath and in this extreme panicking time, I found no one who could help me for nearly hours. I cursed my cousins to the core but more than that about what they must be cooking about me to my parents and other family members. Just then a lorry driver accepts my offer and brings me here to this Dhaba. As soon as the lorry stopped, I jumped off my seat and quenched my thirst with a whole jug of water. It was then I realized that I'm in a totally wrong place and now going back home was a latter concern as my safety was at toss. I went and approached the man who brought me here and asked him if he was going to help me out. He shook his head and handed me to Santoshbaba and told him to just take care of me and that is all I remember of that disastrous day that changed my life to this. Bhaiya I tried endless ways to get away from here but then I felt lost completely and had no option but to return back. I know my parents must have tried every possible means to dig each corner around for me and I'm sure the cousins would have confessed their prank as well as they never would have wanted I would be in such a trouble. But now this is all I have Bhaiya. It's been nearly three years I'm here and this long period is enough for anyone to believe that if someone is absent for so long, he is surely dead." Saying so Bhanu bursts in long and loud sobs as if he never cried so long and deep in last eight years of his changed life. Aaditya was in wet eyes too as all that he could do was consoling Bhanu for his emotional distortion.

"Bhanu..." "Wait Bhaiya, I want to reveal my real name to you, my name is Vansh." Aaditya takes a deep sigh and lays Bhanu's head on his shoulder. Vansh now felt totally empty as he had a catharsis of his woes for the first time.

"Vansh, I'm highly upset and at the same time proud of you that you came this long all on your own and still found joy in your ways of life. I want to tell you something. Can I?" Vansh then raises his head and looks in Aaditya's eyes as the dawn arrived.

"I have now understood you are not made for this life. The more you stretch here, the worse days you face. I'm now close to you. You could consider me your elder brother, your friend, your guide. I'm always there for you but I can also judge and assume that there is nothing for you here.

With this Aaditya takes a pause and Vansh waiting in anticipation for his next utterance desperately looks at him and asks, "What Bhaiya, please tell me."

"Look Vansh, I didn't tell you but I saw my past and childhood in your present. It cropped interest in me and I had an urge to know you and what your past is about. I maintained a rapport with you and now since I know your current condition, I can't let you live here anymore. I know it might be too early to make a decision like this but Vansh I want to take you along with me. I want you to live a better life rather a lavish life, something you deserve. Vansh, I lost my parents too when I was young and I struggled to live on my own but times changed. I was adopted by a very good human. He has riches to rear many more such kids like us and still be happy and called rich. So, I too want you to be a part of our small family. Come with me and you shall never repent your decision. I shall be your brother and all those roles you have been missing in your life. My dad will love you too. Come on Vansh."

Vansh had a mixed potpourri of emotions. He didn't know how to react. He was afraid of Santoshbaba's reaction, he was very happy to meet Aaditya, he was nervous thinking if he would be able to cope up with the new life. With so much of combat in his mind he stands up from his place and tells Aaditya, "Let's go Bhaiya, I want to live my life." Aaditya smiles widely and hugs Vansh and runs to Shiva who was already fixing the car with the help of the Road Assistance team.

"Shiva, are we ready to go?"

"Yes sir, just cleaning the car. It would take..."

"No" interrupted Aaditya, "We got no time. I have a surprise for Dad. Take us home Shiva and yes meet my brother Vansh." Shiva baffled with the statement still smiles in formality.

AFTER A FEW HOURS...

The car enters the Singhania mansion and Vansh had a jaw dropping expression on his face to see where they just entered. It was like a Dream for him to see and accept that he was going to be a part of this life now and what he saw was just the beginning.

As the car stops in front of the house, Vansh and Aaditya look at each other and exchange smiles.

****

I.Q

I.Q.

The alarm clock struck 7 in the morning and a cute little moppet drags himself out of the blanket turning the clock head off. Unwilling to get off his bed, he throws himself on it again until he hears the heavy footsteps of his mother climbing to his room. As soon as he senses the arrival closer he breaks his cocoon and runs off to the bathroom to escape bombarding.

The picture of the room is a total menace. Things scattered hither and thither, clothes dumped in a corner or coming in one's way like a waste or rags. Toys and comics lay like toppings of colourful sprinklers on a cake. But of this entire mess there was a place which was neatly done. It had a chess game on the table which was made of crystal glass displayed as in vintage shops just to add beauty and embellish the place but not for sale. There is a pile of nearly 5 to 6 more chess board games which were packed and thoroughly taken care as if it was a collection hobby.

"Oh! Allah, Imran, Are you there? "How long would you take to finish your shower? You are not getting married today, alright? Come downstairs for breakfast in next 5 minutes or you skip your meals today." That was Shahin, Imran's mother. Like a maternal figure she was just too sensitive about Imran and his advancing career. She wanted to be sure he is actively a part of the rat-race and that she could flaunt and brag about her son's outstanding performance in academics. Shahin belonged to a cliché class of women who yearn and long for a boy child at the first place and if they possess one, he is always on the edge of the sword to prove his intelligence or I.Q.

"Imran Qureshi, Imran Qureshi!" shouted the Teacher. "YES SIR" answered Imran out of a quick but late response. "What do you do always to miss your roll call, Imran? I called out your name twice but you were drowned with your friend in that thing under your desk. Can you do the courteous act of displaying that distraction to public please? Oh! Let me guess is it again your crazy paper chess board game that is driving you bonkers, kid?

As the teacher advances towards his seat, Imran in nervousness slips the sheet underneath the bench space and stands up with alertness. "I'm, I'm sorry sir, please forgive my negligence this time. I abide, I shall hereby adhere to the rules of the class and..." Imran takes a pause, "And...What? Could you accomplish a complete statement Imran?" "And sir I shall play chess only in my Break time." Annoyed by his words as the Teacher frowns and tries to begin a scornful speech, the Recess alarm strikes and Imran apologizes in haste and takes his Board back and runs off with his team mates.

Terribly annoyed with Imran's behavior Mr. Murthy, Imran's math teacher immediately goes to Mr. Joseph who was Imran's class teacher and also pampered his kids a lot. He was quite dear to Imran and vice versa. "Joseph!" uttered Mr. Murthy. "Oh! Mr. Murthy. Now what happened. Again a prank and you are out of your temper, isn't it? Mr. Joseph replied in a light way. "Yes, certainly but this time there is more to it and I felt I should tell you about it since the bond between you and the children is more profound, especially with Imran." Mr. Joseph makes a confused expression and asks Mr. Murthy, "What about him?" "He is just not attentive. I feel his career and studies are in jeopardy. In the past few weeks, he has just been buried under the desk with that brat named Alok. Both chess freaks have just been a nuisance in my class and I'm sure they are not aware from your notice too on this. Am I right, Joseph?" inquired Mr. Murthy.

"Mr. Murthy I guess you are concerned and oblivious of the doomed state their studies might be in due to this casual attitude."

"Yes, you are correct. Before we just lose that decent, obedient and a good student in Imran, we have to take a call. What is distracting him? Why a brain teasing game all the time. Please get into the gist of it and let me know if you need any assistance."

"Sure Mr. Murthy, I'm grateful to you that you noticed this change and answered my doubts."

The next day as Imran entered the class, he found that Alok's place was switched to another row and he was announced to be on a permanent seating right in front of the teachers. Mr. Joseph looked like an enemy and an unpredictable human to Imran. He never expected Mr. Joseph would be so harsh on him after knowing his passion and craze for Chess. Other fellow students could be good friends but not great friends and chess partners which Alok was. Mr. Joseph and Imran talked with their eye contacts. Some blank stares or some glares or a normal gaze at each other. Their minds talked and could pass messages without any verbal discussion. They were that close. That day as Imran went home he felt like slouching and lied like a sandbag on his bed gazing at the ceiling. Just then the doorbell rang. "Hi Dear, Come, how are you?" Shahin welcomed the guest. He is upstairs. Just go. A little puzzled Imran sat upright and gets prepared.

“Hey”. “Oh! Alok. You are here at this time? Surprising! Is everything Ok?” asked Imran.

“Well I was a little curious to know if you have any idea why we both are switched. I mean I didn’t expect this from Mr. Joseph” inquired Alok.

“Yes you are right, me too. I couldn’t keep up my spirits. We haven’t played a single game today. I don’t know if it’s abnormal Alok but I can’t concentrate fully on my studies since my mom has stopped me from playing chess or participating in tournaments. Those competitions kept me going, you know like energy boosters. I very much wanted to enroll for the upcoming National Chess Championship. It would have been the best place to pour our gaming skills Alok.”

There was so much of spark and zest in Imran’s voice just by the mere talk about Chess but with the reality creeping in he could just make an expression of sadness and severe pain.

“See Imran, I know you are very upset. Why don’t you just try talking to your parents, like your Dad? I know he is fine with Chess and you, isn’t he?” proposed Alok.

“He is a very understanding father and I know mom too is just emotional when it’s my studies but I shall try once. I don’t want to diddle myself by keeping it all within and ruin my career.”

In the school, as Imran was walking in the school corridor someone holds him from his shoulder and as he turns he finds no one else but Mr. Joseph.

“I need to have a word with you Imran. Come this way.” Imran followed as if a tamed pet would follow its owner. They reached the OAT of the school where there was a scene of kids playing football in the playground just at a farther distance.

After a few minutes of no word Mr. Joseph breaks the silence and says, "Imran I have been checking you, your sudden and drastic change in behavior, I felt the need to bring you in solace because I want to know what is leading to all this. As much as I know, I am assuming that you too have restrained from your chess play at home. Is that the reason?" Not getting a reply, Mr. Joseph turns to attend Imran who was hiding his face between his folded knees. Mr. Joseph goes closer and puts his hand on his head. "Tell me child what is bothering you. Your grades have descended. You are now a worry to your teachers. What is going wrong Imran? Are you not degrading your I.Q. It's a concern for us, for me."

Imran gathered courage and told everything to Mr. Joseph that entire talk he shared with Alok. He felt so relieved after sharing it all to him and Mr. Joseph just had a line to say, "We will do something about it, Imran." Saying so Imran and Mr. Joseph walked back to the classroom. On the way back Imran is agile and smiling, lagging his hand to Mr. Joseph with so much affection. That day Imran had acquired special permission to stay at Alok's for a study meet and his mom had agreed, Alok was noticing Imran's face.

As they began their game of the day, Alok couldn't resist asking him, "Something has happened today at school? You look so light and happy. Seems your mom agreed. Is it?" Imran not losing that positivity replied, "No, not really but I had a talk with Mr. Joseph at school and I felt so good Alok. I'm sure he would get a way out of this maze for me." "Wow that's amazing. There wouldn't be greater news if your parents allow you for the tournament."

On his way back home Imran had his brain overcrowded with so many dreams and in this period he reaches home and rings the doorbell. To his surprise his mom comes smiling towards him, welcomes him and takes him inside where he finds Mr.

Joseph sitting with his father. Imran was clueless of the entire scenario in front of him. In a jiffy, he could unriddle that the smiling faces meant some good news is waiting for him and as he brooded on it.

Mr. Aasif Qureshi calls Imran closer and tells him, "Mr. Joseph came and assured us that chess will not be a distraction for you. You can participate in the tournament my son." Imran starts smiling in joy and looks at everyone when his mother says, "Yes but you have to prove that we made a right decision for us and you too." Imran falls on his mom's lap and hugs her tight saying, "I promise Mummy."

And for Mr. Joseph all he could do was saying "Thankyou sir, Thanks a lot." Mr. Joseph informed Imran that he just got the tournament form signed by his parents and just needed that one favour from Imran and that was his outstanding performance. Imran affirmed their expectation with a firm look.

After a week when Imran's final tests were over and his long awaited wish was about to come true he and Alok held each other's hands and wish luck at the Chess tournament. Imran had promised himself to try all his skills in the game not to regret later. After a whole day's continuous gaming and exchanging of participants the last round, the Final round for the tournament was to be played which comprised of two teams which had Alok and the other participant and the other team of Imran and a girl participant. The competition was a tough one as it had master in it. It went on for a long time and when both the teams declared check mate it was a great feeling of achievement. The results were to be declared. Imran, Alok and the other two participants stood like plastic mannequins on the stage waiting for their acknowledgements. Mr. Joseph, Imran's parents, Alok's parents had occupied a row in the front so that they wouldn't miss a bit of the moment of victory of their wards. As the judges announced the prizes the other two participants were declared on the third and fourth position. Now, it was a relief that either Alok or Imran was going to be the Lucky one.

Alok and Imran stood there holding hands. They were happy within. They tried, played and came this far and that was their biggest reward. As they kept waiting in anticipation the judges announced that Alok was on the second position and Imran owned the First Prize. The overwhelmed panel of Alok and Imran family couldn't resist climbing the stage and Mr. Joseph just stood down there in tears clapping hard for Imran. He was so glad Imran made him proud and more than that he proved his promise right. As Imran was being felicitated with a scholarship of one lakh he called Mr. Joseph on the stage to share his Prize. The crowd applauded this emotional moment and everyone congratulated Imran and Alok for their success and for letting their school's and parent's name high. The entire scene looked like a great celebration indeed. The kids were joyous and vain that they could get a chance to do what they wanted to do. They could show their skills and be paid for it.

The next day at the school Imran and his parents were seated waiting for Imran's Report card. Shahin was too restless and curious about Imran's result. Now, when Alok and his parents left and the four were alone, Mr. Joseph called Imran and his parents. As they sat on the bench everybody was eyeing the hand movements of Mr. Joseph, turning pages of Imran's report card.

"Imran, this is your Result card. Please see it thoroughly." Saying so Mr. Joseph looks at his parents which added more stress to them.

"Imran what is your result. Could you just tell us?" Shahin jolted Imran and insisted him continuously. Imran looks at his mother with a blank face without uttering a word. "I knew it. I told you not to allow him for this tournament, I regret my decision and he made us feel shameful. I knew he would flunk. I told..." as Shahin kept talking, Imran hands over his result to her and Shahin with that scornful look snatches it from him and to her shock she finds that Imran stood second in the whole class and he made an outstanding come back. Alok stood first and topped the section. Shahin and Mr. Aasif were moved to see Imran's numbers and all they could do was apologize to him and Sir Joseph for underestimating their abilities. Imran held his head high and now he could multi task his skill and studies very well. He was a mark of strength for his folks, friends and teachers. He was proud and confident. Happy and content. He breathed deeply and hugged Mr. Joseph. Now, Imran's parent's stood there watching the student teacher bond and let them walk by to spend some motivational time.

****

FIRST CRUSH

FIRST CRUSH

"Dear Students, thank you for choosing me the Head Boy for the coming year as well. I promise I will prove myself again and will not let you down. I'm really thankful to all those who put trust and confidence in me and my work for our school. Together we will go far. Thank you again."

As this thanksgiving speech was over, Dev was climbing down the stairs to join his fellow mates with pride; the school auditorium was filled with hooting and screams congratulating his victory. Out of thousands of students who supported him, there was a shy, coy and humble student in the girl's crowd, who couldn't resist eyeing Dev and his smile, his aura, his fan following, the way he was being cheered and praised by his teachers. She felt in a total awe of this boy. His confidence, the way he approached others, his dutiful attitude all this caught her attention on her inaugural day at St. Thomas School, Mumbai.

Kaya had enrolled herself in the school for her junior college career. It was her first assembly which gave her a lively vibe as a part of the school. Kaya, happy with her academics, faculties, classmates and a few friends began enjoying this session of her life. She was not too attentive to Dev as a classmate but they exchanged smiles on seldom basis.

It was just then after a few weeks; kaya was a little late for her practical. As she was about to rush for the same and started crossing the class corridor, a piece of paper drew her attention. As soon as she picked it up to read, she found it saying Dev, you are my first crush. Revealing these words in mind kaya was extremely cautious and she thought the best to do with the paper was to destroy it. She did not realize when out of her own carelessness it slipped out and it was on the corridor floor. Fortunately, it was in her own hands so that she can bury it forever.

As soon as she was about to crumple the paper, she realized someone was just behind her and the voice uttered, "Excuse me". Kaya extremely frightened, crushes the paper, turns back and throws it in the lawn next to the corridor. As she turns she finds to her fright that it was none other than Dev himself. What is she going to do now? She had made it obvious by her expressions and pale face that she engaged into something strange. But Dev couldn't grasp the reality and asked, "You are the new comer right? What is your name? Kaya had never faced Dev so closely. All she could do as the most courageous act was to smile at him from a distance and that made her day. So she was totally lost and blocked how to react. She kept staring at him with a fear of busting the reality and suddenly Dev again repeats saying, "Hey! Are you alright?" You seem to be sick. You need some help?" Kaya gaining some normality looks into his eyes and says, "I'm Kaya and I'm just fine. I just got late for my pratical classes so..."

"That's fine. I was on a check and saw you so thought of helping you. You seem to have missed the school tour because the Practical classes are on the other side. This area usually leads to the garden for a stress relieving walk and OAT a little ahead. Anyway, so let's begin from here itself as it would be easier for you to recollect.

As Dev and Kaya start walking, there was someone examining kaya before Dev reached out for her. Seemed someone was trying to meet her when she was alone and that someone lost this opportunity.

Dev and Kaya got a little friendly by the end of the school tour. Kaya was at ease with Dev being next to him now and her liking had now turned stronger. She liked Dev's other side as a person. She wanted to be more of a good friend now with him and after the trip was almost done they came to the practical class corridor to find that the classes had been extended. Now, Dev too had begun engaging in off track talks and knowing more about Kaya.

Both of them were unaware of the fact that they are not alone, and the stranger kept waiting till the two returned back. They indulged in some light talks and giggle to it. Just then Kaya slips her foot off the steps and loses her control to fall down. Looking at this, Dev as a sudden reaction gushes to hold her and abruptly from behind the garden wall springs up a boy. Both the boys caught hold of Kaya. The trio gazed at one another totally unaware how to react. For kaya the third person was a complete stranger and that made her numb and for Dev the boy was none other than his one-year elder brother named Aatish from the same school. It was pretty embarrassing for Aatish since he never wanted to appear in front of Kaya this way.

Now, as the three of them were balanced, they decided to meet after the school departure as Kaya wanted to run away from the entire scene that took place. As planned they met at the school playground where usually Dev and Aatish spent their post school hours gossiping and teasing with their buddies.

"Look I want to say something before any one of you ask me what I was doing behind the garden wall", proposed Aatish.

Dev and Kaya were eagerly waiting for Aatish to break the secret.

"This might sound too rough and candid but I want to confess that I have a crush on Kaya since I saw her. Her simplicity and innocence made me admire her personality. Today I was awaiting a chance to have a word with her to be friends with me but Dev your sudden entry spoilt it all and I had to run to hold Kaya while she tripped from the stairs. That is all I wanted to say. But the bizarre thing was Kaya indulged into something that changed her total attitude in a jiffy and before I could figure it out, I picked up the note she discarded and trashed in the garden. As I opened the chit I found..."

"Excuse me both of you I have to rush home as my mother would be worrying why I am behind time today. So please allow me to exit this conversation." Dev barges in and says, "Hold on Kaya. Please forgive me but I can feel you are unwilling to announce the truth in the card and I am quite inquisitive about what was inside it. Now that we are decent friends I'd at least expect that favour from both of you.

Kaya was in a dilemma as she adored Dev as a friend more now and with the content unfolded she might lose him forever in every way and there was a rare possibility that he'd respect that part of her emotions. Moreover, Dev was already in a shock hearing about the infatuation his brother had towards her and so was Kaya.

"Kaya, Dev. Let's not make things difficult. Kaya you don't need to bother about what Dev would think of you once he knows of the letter, it is quite normal and we are now friends and I can see this friendship among the three of us going a long way. So let me go forth saying the letter said Kaya had the First crush on you, Dev."

With these words kaya started breathing deeply than normal and her face drowned with insecurity. Unable to react immediately, Dev took a little instance and then looked at Aatish and they nodded at each other. Now, the brothers put their hands forth to her and as she felt this reaction she grew her face up and looked at the two of them. They just smiled at Kaya and initiated the word together, "FRIENDS?" Kaya a little submissive and patient brooded a little and broke the seriousness, smiled and advanced her hands to each one and replied with a wide smile saying, "BEST FRIENDS."

The new friendship had now begun its journey for a long way.

****

THE TEN O' CLOCK TRAIN

THE TEN O'CLOCK TRAIN

Raghav and Nandi got into a wedlock just a few months back through a normal traditional manner. A proper arranged wedding. Despite being a new company the two hardly took time getting into bondage. They cherished their company and just had real love to give each other. They were always talked by the people about their togetherness. They promised not to separate in the worst times.

But today Raghav stood alone at the railway station waiting with a desperate heart to receive Nandi who was to return from her parent's home after three days of stay. He never thought he will have to live without her even a day. He was prepared for the time he had set in his mind and it was taking a little longer for Nandi to return back to her marital life.

As Raghav was musing about her, a male voice shouts his name, "Raghu?"

As Raghu turns back he finds his friend Ishwar waving with a smile. Raghav trying hard to manage a fake smile goes forth and hugs him.

"It's good to see you dear. I just returned from a small trip with my wife. It was a great time. She's here." Ishwar calls out her name.

"Meet my wife Raksha. Raksha, He is Raghav my dear friend." Raksha smiles and bids a Namaste to Raghav and they exchanged smiles.

"What are you doing here, where is Nandi?" Questioned Ishwar.

"She's supposed to return today by the ten o'clock train but she hasn't returned yet so I am waiting to receive her." Raghav shares while turning his head again and again waiting to see if Nandi's train had arrived.

"Oh, so you must be very excited then. Let us not disturb you. You continue and we shall meet up once you are free and with Nandi."

Ishwar smiles and leaves with his wife.

Now Raghav is watching the two of them walk away, holding hands, giggling and tugged close while walking. This reminds him of Nandi and his times. He remembers the new days of their marriage and togetherness. How they were both happy only in each other's company. Just talked and confessed love and adored their presence. While thinking of it he started recollecting all about Nandi and her charm. Her features had luster even without a slightest make up. Her allurement was natural and deep. Such a sparkling appearance one could hardly resist appreciating. Raghav could just spend hours sitting and just praising her dark, thick and intense locks, her lips that were so perfectly shaped like a newly bloomed rose bud, and her eyes that spoke a thousand words without uttering them and that were worth an endless gaze, her entire face which formed symmetry with a smooth and delicate layer of a fresh and pure skin tone that needed no add on. Her hair strands that kept falling on her face like the night covers the day. Nandi had the charisma to appeal in her to magnetize Raghav so much close, he could hardly indulge in else. Sometimes they would just stare at each other and express their feelings. Nandi felt she was the most fortunate woman who was loved by Raghav more than she could even imagine. Nandi and Raghav just had tones of love and affection to give one another. The rest was in place.

The clock struck eleven and it made a big alarm announcing the arrival of the next train. Raghav with a rush ran to the platform and started searching everywhere if Nandi was in this train. He looked at the faces of each female who got off the train but he failed to find her. After the entire train was off board, he gave up on his efforts to wait for her. With a heavy heart he returns home and sees his folks waiting to greet and receive Nandi after her arrival. But after knowing of no news they pacified Raghav and convinced him to go and check for her tomorrow at the same time.

"May be she decided to stay back more or may be one of her parents are ill and they need her? Think positive. Don't worry my son she will return to you. Have faith", said Raghav's father Sikanderji.

Raghav and Nandi had no way to communicate either as they used the coin phone booth to pass messages or letters initially when they were not married. As Raghav got this thought in his mind he rose and started running to the station where he knew his uncle had a phone booth which he used to talk to her sometimes.

"Raghu, where are you going?" shouted his mother and father with an upright position in alarm.

"I will be back. I need to make a phone call." shouted back Raghav.

With all the energy he ran to the booth and took out his small diary he always carried with him which had all important numbers, address and records.

He started dialing the number quickly with trembling hands hoping to get an answer. It was the number of Nandi's neighbor who was a close family to hers and it was the most convenient way to talk to her. He was in the course of thoughts as to how he forgot this connection to reach her and while thinking so the other side went unanswered. Raghav tried the number numerous times but didn't receive an answer. He was so upset and low that he started walking towards his home in haste and on the way he wept with loud screams expressing Nandi's separation.

"I couldn't get a response from Gupta uncle, Papa. I think there is something wrong with Nandi and her family and it's not giving me a good vibe." expressed Raghav.

Raghav's mother started crying to his words and looking at her Sikanderji went to Raghav and told him, "Raghu, I can understand that you have lost hopes after these efforts. I can see that you are trying hard to find Nandi's location but you need to be strong. As I said there must be some reason why she hasn't come back."

To this Raghav with a desperate tone says," Yes, Papa that is what I am wondering that if she is stuck with something she should at least give a call and inform us. It's just next to her house."

"I agree that is a concern. Let's wait for tomorrow night's ten o'clock train and if not we shall go to Nandi's home and fetch her but as of now be sane and look after yourself and feed yourself as you are empty since morning." concluded Sikanderji.

The next morning Raghav again goes to the booth and gives a call to Gupta uncle but to his hard luck it went unanswered too. He was now sitting under the shade of a tree near the station throwing stones at a close distance and trying to kill time. He had a pale skin now, dry lips because of thirst and drowsy eyes showing he didn't sleep at all. He had to keep up till ten o' clock as it was the hope that kept him alive. He couldn't imagine his life without Nandi and if it happened he had decided a cruel end to his existence.

As time passed it was now late evening and Raghav stood there in curiosity for the train's arrival.

"Oh Lord! If I ever loved Nandi truly and if she did the same, please let my wait and despair cease tonight and I believe the faith I possess in you and also that you won't let it go futile." talked Raghav to his supreme power.

Here's the whistle of the ten o'clock train. Finally, it was there again. People getting off the train, rushing out, pushing each other with no patience. It was bursting with passengers and it was a hindrance for Raghav to pull his neck and find Nandi but still he managed to look every compartment that emptied but it didn't work. He couldn't find Nandi again. He didn't see her glimpse. He also thought that she might have walked ahead so he ran back to the other end but all in vain. What was he supposed to do now" Leave or wait? He was getting mad and sick of this failure and in this messed up state he sat down on a bench and started sobbing. Raghav had given up his hopes on Nandi and then suddenly as he sat there lonely, weak and sad with his neck laid on the bench head he heard someone shouting his name loudly.

"Raghu, Raghu!" It was Ishwar his friend whom Raghav saw running towards him with unusual energy. He couldn't guess the reason behind it and didn't bother to look at him any further. But Ishwar came close to him lacking breath and saying, "Raghu, get up just get up. What are you doing here?"

"Ishwar just leave me alone. I want to go nowhere. I will come once I feel like, so please inform Maa." replied Raghav.

"Raghu, you are dumb I think. Come with me idiot it's very important."

Raghav look at him with annoyance and says, "What is it Ishwar? You already must know my wife hasn't returned since two days and I am unable to trace her anywhere, I don't know if she is ok, if she is far or if she is... Alive." saying so Raghav falls on Ishwar's shoulder and cries. Ishwar holds his head and tells him, "Raghu that is what I am telling you my friend. Nandi is Alive. She is fine and..." Before Ishwar could complete his sentence Raghav springs up from the bench and looks at Ishwar with those red, wet eyes and holds his hand tight and runs with him as fast as he could. While running he was so overwhelmed that he yelled in extreme joy and asked Ishwar, "Where is she?" Ishwar said, "Just come with me."

They now stop at Raghav's uncle's phone booth and Ishwar pointed at Nandi who had covered her face with a translucent dupatta. As Raghav advanced to see her, he could see Nandi's minor face details through the dupatta. As Raghav elevated her dupatta he just couldn't react or proceed and got an eyeful of Nandi with helplessness and moisture in his eyeballs and his lips sealed with his palms. Nandi raised her face to have a sight of her husband's face and as she does so the two had the same state of feelings.

Nandi with a grieving look and a fast throbbing heart gives a stare at Raghav. The depth of their misery was similar. The pain they felt was ditto. The days were two but at the bottom the bliss they perceived was indescribable. Raghu caressed her hair and cheeks, those scars and bruises. He was happy beyond explanation as he touched her innocence again. He fell in love with that self of her too. He could just stop that time to record the moment of their patch up. They couldn't curb their desire and fused into a passionate embrace in front of Ishwar and Khalil Chacha who brought Nandi all the way to be with Raghav. After they were cured of their sorrow, Nandi now wiped her eyes and Raghav's too and looked at him saying, "Let me tell you how all this happened Raghav.

We were heading to a temple in a mini bus and unfortunately the bus met with a severe accident. Maa, Baba, me, Gupta uncle's family and other people too in the bus were injured badly. We needed medical help immediately but we were not in a state to do so. Thanks to Khalil Chacha who stopped by and saw the scene and immediately brought help else I would have been in a serious state. I had no other help Raghav to come to you so I asked Khalil Chacha if he could just drop me to you and how thankful I am that I found him else we might not have seen each other again Raghu for some more time until you came there to fetch me." saying so Nandi looks at Khalil Chacha and smiles.

"Chacha I can't tell you the happiness your act of humanity has brought me and many other lives. I was in a terrible position without Nandi; we were all too stressed about her and now that she's back to me I will never let her go alone anywhere and I am sure I love her much more now as her worth is priceless for me." Expressing his gratitude Raghav hugs Khalil Chacha and he returns it too.

"My dear child I saw that Nandi's love and dedication for you is so deep and profound I had no other way but to attend it. If not, I would have died of the guilt of not helping so many people who were suffering. After seeing both of you unite I feel so proud to be the medium of making it possible. God bless you both and I wish you both never depart."

Raghav and Nandi take Chacha's blessings, thank Ishwar and start their little journey to their home hand in hand, smiling and just justifying their reunion.

****

THE LAST PHOTOGRAPH

THE LAST PHOTOGRAPH

Sora reads the letter from a renowned and well known photographer complimenting her photography skills and her opportunistic art of capturing the best moments in anything that she chooses. She just smiles on the mention of these words by her own mentor.

Sora Marc, daughter of an Indo-Western couple always aspired to be a great photographer. After she won the award for the candid shot category she was highly appreciated everywhere both nationally as well as internationally. Sora wanted to do something out of the way to create a moment that was indeed captivating and hence she thought of the spontaneous and natural smile of a child. Basically from the US, Sora decided to travel to Mumbai and search for that perfect smile in the slum areas of the local streets of the metro and how well she knew her thoughts, she found it and got the acknowledgement she deserved. She was getting calls from her country and everyone was pouring good words and wishes to her in different forms. She was extremely happy to have reached a level higher in her passion of being one of the best photographers.

While thinking of all the fame and goodness god had showered upon her, Zeba her assistant informs her saying, "Sora, this is it. Apart from all that you are hearing right now I am sure you don't want to lose on this."

Sora looks at her and asks, "What is it?" she smiles while sipping her coffee and adds, "Is my desired challenge on Best Photograph announced?"

"Yes, you are right." replies Zeba.

The long wait for Sora was over. All these years she had made a great name in this industry but she deeply longed for this one category which was her last felt dream to be fulfilled. She wanted this day since the time she started this profession.

She goes forth to Zeba and holds her arms tight and hugs her. "I am so happy. This is it Zeba. I can now step still by producing the best of my work and outshine the others. I have to do this; I have to grab this one to be on the top of the list. Start looking for locations right away, I don't have time to waste.

Zeba assures her to find the choicest location for the game. The Sponsors of the event were providing every financial support to the participants. They just had to choose any spot, reach there, explore and click a photograph worth to fit in the category of the championship.

Sora was deeply visualizing the frame of her snap just then she gets a ring from her Mother.

"Hi mom, sorry I couldn't talk to you all this time as it was all too hectic here for me working on the click but finally I made it. I hope now you and Dad won't regret my decision of this choice of career."

During the call, Zeba enters and asks her to give a minute.

"Mom, I will give you a call back sooner, do give my love to Dad and I will see both of you very soon, I Love you mom, Bye."

"Yes Zeba. Where are we going?"

"I had short listed a few places but seems most of them have opted for the commonest sites. I think we could go for one unmentioned venue and it is the African forests. What do you think?"

"Nice.", replies Sora. "Where I could capture the uncommon breeds of creatures or the tribal race or may be something unexplored?"

"Sora, you have the skill of finding the rare in the common thing, I surely don't doubt you will make a spectacular form of your preference. You are the creator of your own opportunity. Should I freeze the location and begin the formalities to move for the trip?" inquires Zeba.

"Well, I agree to your words and I guess I will crop the real moment where I get an instinct. Let's go for it."

So the African Jungle was Sora's place of purpose, a purpose that she had to turn into her achievement.

When Sora landed she had a person to receive her from the crew. She was given a good welcome and wasting not a moment she was taken to the African Forest. As she entered the woods she was stunned and extremely pleased to see how blessed is the land of Africa with so much nature and lush tone of green everywhere she looked. She chose to put up her tent in the forest for a day as she was quite assertive of digging out the superlative click in the forest in that span.

With the help of the forest crew Sora gets settled at a safe place but couldn't resist her urge to begin hunting for her scene. So she moves to the forest's heart watching birds, animals secretly, chose their postures and clicked them. She found a lot of eye capturing animals like African Civet. The peculiar species of birds like the long tailed hombills, bongo antelopes, crowned eagles, hyenas, zebras, vultures but of all these she waited for that unusual and rare moment inclusive of an outstanding click.

Apart from the wild life animals she also spotted some African tribal people hunting for their living. There came a state where Sora and a tribal woman with her child was eye-to-eye. The woman was a little frightened to see her but when she indicated the camera and revealed her other snapshots she had, the woman smiled and took Sora by her hand to her other tribe folks. Here she encountered huts so beautifully designed and handmade, crafted with proper dome that was covered with the dry but fine and thin leaf stalks. This African tribe had little children, women, men and even aged members. Each dressed in a traditional form. The women with the new born wore a thin cloth tightly draped around the body and in the same was tugged the child either to the front or the back of the mother assuring safety. The men wore a square piece of material covering the rear part of their bodies and held a long stick with sharp stones tied to their tops which confessed they had self-made weapons for hunting and self-defense. The people tied their hair in crochet braids. Their body ornaments were marvelous which combined a lot of handcrafted jewellery that comprised of metal rings in a tone of gold with different sizes for the neck, ears, hands and feet.

Sora was stunned to view such incredible beauty in every creation of nature. Africa was giving her the incomparable experience as an individual and also as a paparazzo. She clicked so many snaps of the tribal race but out of all that she had, she wasn't convinced to pass any through the top of all. She continued walking ahead now with more desperation and urgency for her shot. She advanced further and immediately hid herself behind a tree. What did she see?

She talked to herself with so much excitement, "This is my trophy winning moment. I kept running in the forest since morning and its right here. Let me set up my camera with the finest lens and I surely can't afford to lose this scene. So rare, unusual and breath taking."

Everything is set up. Sora is ready for the camera take of that still moment that was definitely going to change her life and career. She gives the flawless performance of her art, talent and clicks the image. Before she could miss on it, she runs to her tent checks the quality, angle, and more than anything the content of the still. That was the catch of her workmanship. Sora quickly sends the copy to the official people for the competition. Once she was done, her joy was immeasurable and she could just thank nature for putting this up in front of her.

While she was rejoicing her success in her imagination she reversed her actions and saw that sight again. With that mere thought Sora couldn't control her emotions and she ran with all her potency to go back to that place. When she was running she started cursing herself and her inhuman approach to that sight as it was going to take a life. It was of a group of vultures surrounding a baby and that was clearly untypical for anyone to see and mark notice.

But now Sora had a lineage of all bad thoughts coming to her mind and as she reaches the spot she sees that the vultures had put the little child to death and others too were feeding on it. Looking at that Sora yelled her heart out and she was in acute dismay. Following it she ran back to her tent and gathered up all her belongings and asked the forest crew to set up her return. Now that Sora had been through her task, she was back home with her family, relatives, Zeba and her friends. Everybody was waiting for the results to be out by the jury. When Sora came back to her domicile with her parents in the US, she was too upset and often chose to stay alone with herself. All her friends, family were keen on meeting her after her return but she had withdrawn all her contacts gradually.

After a few days, as Sora was going through the pictures at Africa she had no expressions to feel. She couldn't cover up the guilt that kept piling inside her for not saving the child. The hunger of fame and success was so deeply intoxicated in her that her humanity was far to be exhibited at that moment. Now, she came across the photo she was sure of naming her the winner. The shot clearly showed the vulture tempting eyes on the child's fresh flesh and blood. She saw the naivety and purity in the child's eyes. It was chubby, dark, had curly hair and it viewed the vultures around itself. Looking at this helplessness, Sora tore off all the pictures and outraged her sorrow.

While she was sobbing she gets a call from Zeba saying, "Sora, Are you there?"

"Yes Zeba, what happened? Have the results come out for the Awards?"

"Yes, Sora you are correct and as you can guess my joyous voice you have excelled this rivalry by standing on the top with your remarkable talent. You won The Best Photograph trophy Sora. Congratulations. You have achieved everything now and you are the youngest and established photographer. I am so happy for you."

Sora just replies with a pale Thank you to Zeba's reaction and hangs up.

Everyone gets the news about Sora's extraordinary earning and triumph. Sora's parents come upstairs to her room to felicitate her as soon as they get the news but they get no answer from her. As they forge ahead to open the door, to their immeasurable trauma they find Sora hanging to the ceiling fan. She ended her life out of a terrible guilt of not saving a baby's life in the craving for a high acclamation.

Sora couldn't face her inner conscience and decided to feed her guilt by killing her own self. When her parents progressed forth to her body, mourning and weeping, they find the same photograph in her hand with her writing that said "The Last Photograph."

****

9 789354 724831

Printed by Libri Plureos GmbH in Hamburg,
Germany